Abracazebra

Story by
Helen Docherty

Illustrated by
Thomas Docherty

In Yawnalot, a sleepy old place
   Where everyone knew each other's face,
     Life went by in its usual way;
      Day after day . . . after day . . . after day.

The children ran out of things to do,
With nothing exciting and nothing new.
So they'd all sit around and watch old Goat
Patching the holes on his fishing boat.

But then, one evening, a stranger came.

Nobody dared to ask her name.

She came on a bicycle decked with flowers.

(They say she rode for hours and hours.)

She parked her bike in the village square
And started to build a stage – right there.

Word spread fast,
   and the rumours flew.
What *was* this stranger going to do?

Goat sat and sulked by the sycamore tree.
"She doesn't look all that special to me.
A moment ago, they thought *I* was great.
I bet she can't hammer a nail in straight!"

But the crowd in the square continued to swell,
As a drum beat loud and silence fell.
The sky lit up with a fiery glow . . .

MAGIC
SHOW

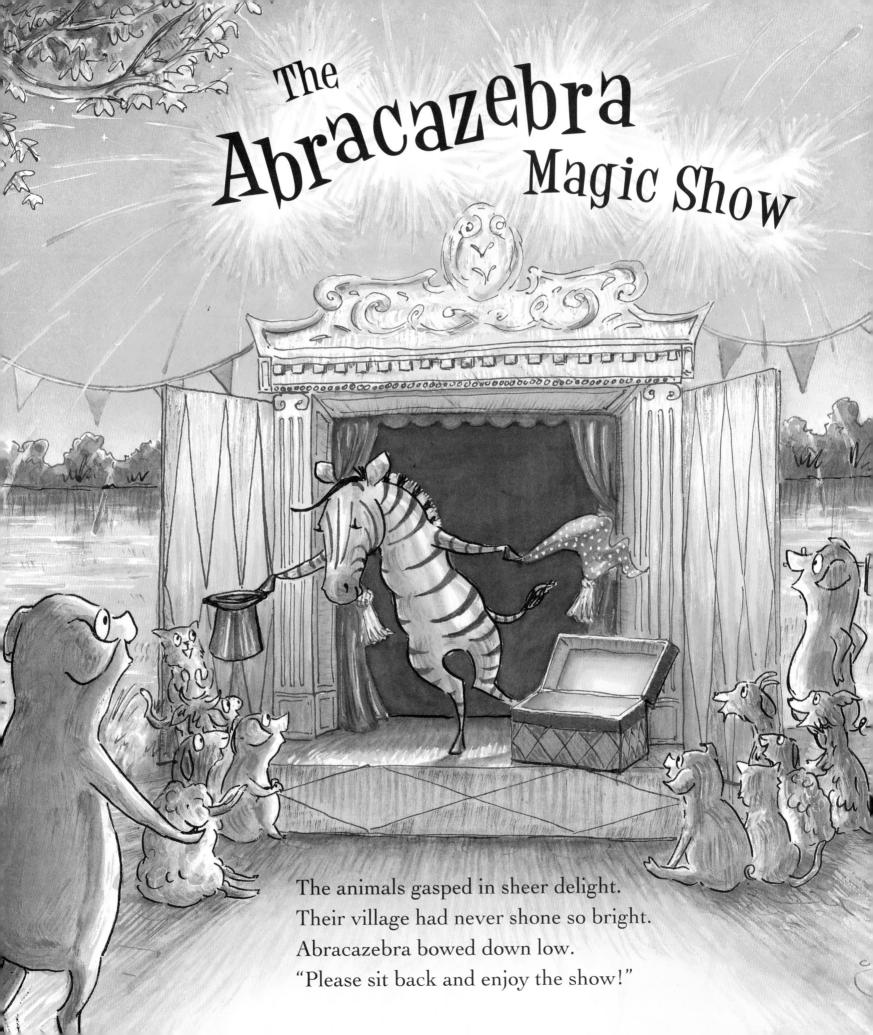

The Abracazebra Magic Show

The animals gasped in sheer delight.
Their village had never shone so bright.
Abracazebra bowed down low.
"Please sit back and enjoy the show!"

A beanstalk grew
   from a tiny bean
   (The tallest stalk
      they'd ever seen);

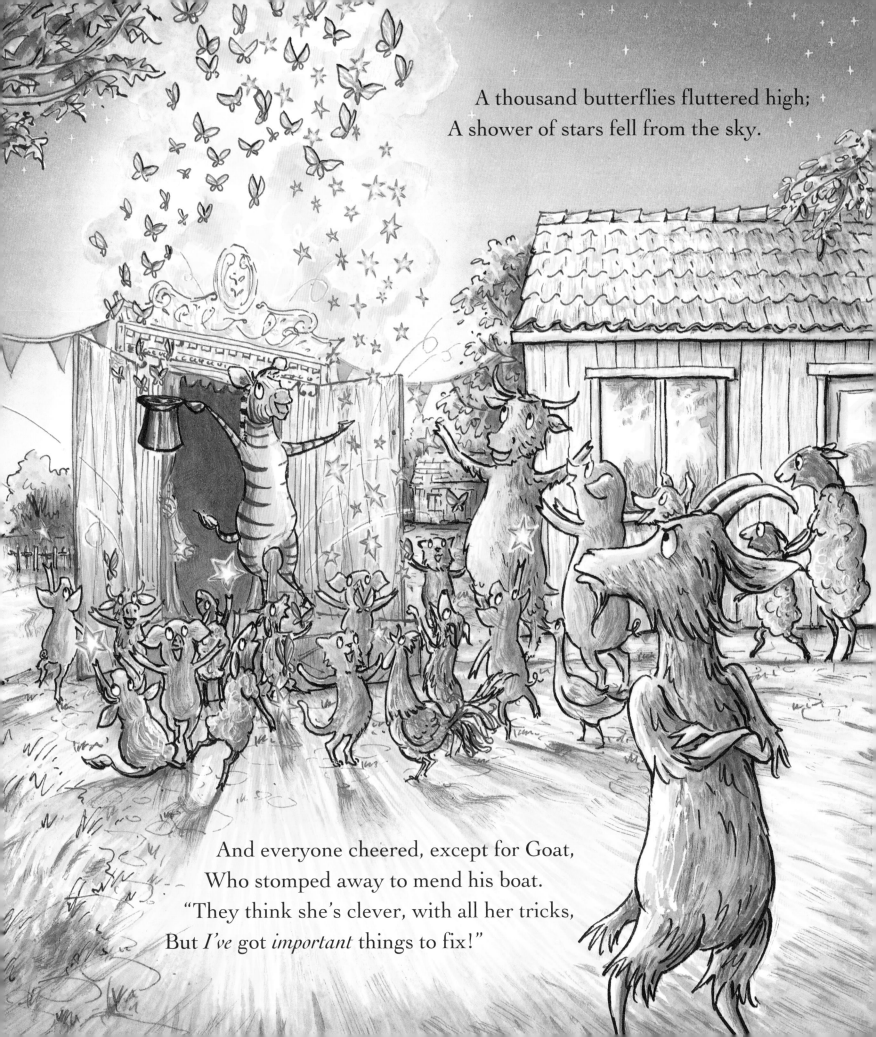

A thousand butterflies fluttered high;
A shower of stars fell from the sky.

And everyone cheered, except for Goat,
Who stomped away to mend his boat.
"They think she's clever, with all her tricks,
But *I've* got *important* things to fix!"

When Abracazebra's show was done,
The animals thanked her, one by one.

Pig brought a jug of lemonade;
Cow brought some biscuits,
freshly made.

Sheep volunteered a bed for the night,
But she smiled and said, "No, I'll be all right.
I'll sleep underneath this sycamore tree.
The grass is a good enough bed for me."

MAGIC
SHOW

For the rest of that week in Yawnalot
The village square was a lively spot,
With new performances every day
And games for the littlest ones to play.

And under the shade of the sycamore tree
Abracazebra spoke of the sea;

Of jungles, hills,
and grassy plains;

Of deserts, where
it never rains;

Of how, after cycling through town after town,
It was time – perhaps – to settle down.

The animals begged,
"Stay here with us!"

But Goat just muttered, "What a fuss
For a few silly stripes and a travelling show.
This Abracazebra has got to go!"

So he started to whisper in people's ears,
Conjuring up their darkest fears:
"*Abracazebra?* I smell a rat.
You can't trust an animal with stripes like that!
You don't see stripes on a pig or a cow . . .

. . . So why should we welcome
stripes here now?"

And, one by one, they all agreed

That she *was* an extra mouth to feed.

And no one complained
(well, not out loud)
When a sign appeared:
"NO STRIPES ALLOWED".

She must have left
before the dawn,

And all (but Goat) felt quite forlorn.
A guilty silence hung in the air,
Now Abracazebra wasn't there.

Then the smallest Kid began to cry,
"Why's Abracazebra gone,
Mum, *why*?"

Goat paced around the sycamore tree.
"*Should* I have made them listen to me?
Maybe she wasn't all that bad.
And now she's gone; and everyone's sad."

He gave his beard a sorry shake.
"I think I've made a big mistake."

He tore the sign from
the sycamore tree.
But where could
Abracazebra be?

"Does anyone know
    which way she went?"
        Dog was the first to find her scent.
            "I think she went down the river track."

"Okay, follow me – we'll get her back!"
The animals all ran after Goat
And clambered into his fishing boat.

They sailed and sailed, while the hot sun shone...
But where had Abracazebra gone?

Then, just when they thought
they could search no more,
They saw her, pedalling by the shore.

Goat leapt up to the river track.
"Abracazebra, please come back!
I'm sorry I made you go away.
We *need* your stripes; so won't you stay?"

Abracazebra smiled at Goat . . .

And climbed down on to his fishing boat.

Now Yawnalot is a happier place
Where they welcome any kind of face.
There's a goat, I'm told, who serves up tea
Under the shade of the sycamore tree.

And Abracazebra?
    Well, if you go . . .

WELCOME

. . . You might just catch her magic show!

WELCOME

For Chloe and Laila,
Ellen and Joe,
Isla and Elsie,
Sofía and Rafael.

First published in 2015 by Alison Green Books
An imprint of Scholastic Children's Books
Euston House, 24 Eversholt Street, London NW1 1DB
A division of Scholastic Ltd
www.scholastic.co.uk
London – New York – Toronto – Sydney – Auckland
Mexico City – New Delhi – Hong Kong

Text copyright © 2015 Helen Docherty
Illustrations copyright © 2015 Thomas Docherty

HB ISBN: 978 1 407145 37 2
PB ISBN: 978 1 407145 38 9